Ken Hops
and
Ken's Plan

'Ken Hops' and 'Ken's Plan'
An original concept by Sheryl Webster
© Sheryl Webster 2023

Illustrated by Yoss Sánchez

Published by MAVERICK ARTS PUBLISHING LTD
Studio 11, City Business Centre, 6 Brighton Road,
Horsham, West Sussex, RH13 5BB
© Maverick Arts Publishing Limited August 2023
+44 (0)1403 256941

A CIP catalogue record for this book is available at the British Library.

ISBN 978-1-84886-974-5

www.maverickbooks.co.uk

Pink

This book is rated as: Pink Band (Guided Reading)
It follows the requirements for Phase 2 phonics.
Most words are decodable, and any non-decodable words are familiar, supported by the context and/or represented in the artwork.

Ken Hops
and
Ken's Plan

By Sheryl Webster

Illustrated by Yoss Sánchez

The Letter k

Trace the lower and upper case letter with a finger. Sound out the letter.

Down, lift, down, down

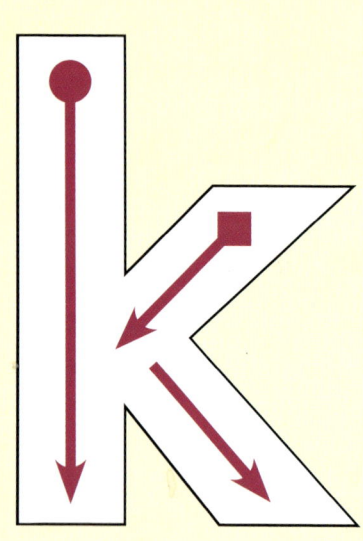

Down, lift, down, down

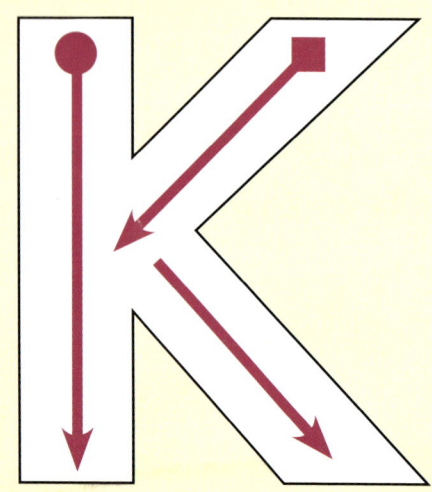

Some words to familiarise:

hopper   over   frog

High-frequency words:

a   up   on

Tips for Reading 'Ken Hops'

- Practise the words listed above before reading the story.
- If the reader struggles with any of the other words, ask them to look for sounds they know in the word. Encourage them to sound out the words and help them read the words if necessary.
- After reading the story, ask the reader who Ken hopped over.

Fun Activity

Discuss which animals can hop!

Ken Hops

Ken cannot hop.

Ken gets a hopper.

Ken can hop!

Ken can hop over Dog.

Ken can hop over Frog.

Ken can hop up... up... up!

POP!

Ken cannot hop.

Ken can hop!

The Letter P

Trace the lower and upper case letter with a finger. Sound out the letter.

*Down,
up,
around*

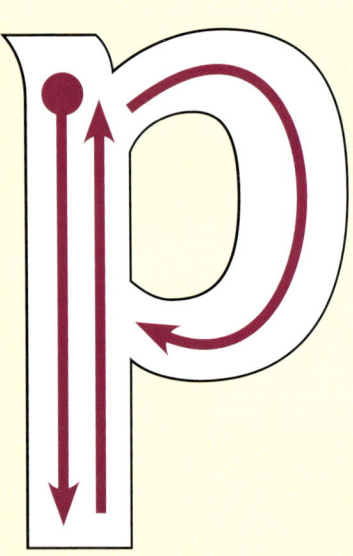

*Down,
up,
around*

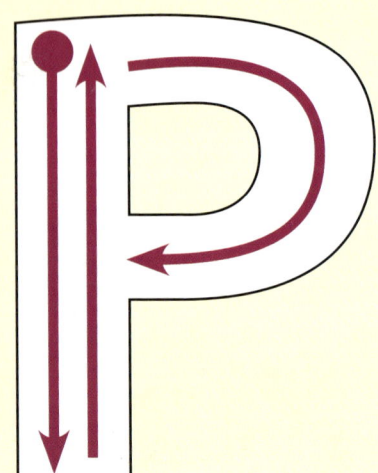

Some words to familiarise:

Ken   spot   Meg

High-frequency words:

it   has   a   go   up

Tips for Reading 'Ken's Plan'

- Practise the words listed above before reading the story.
- If the reader struggles with any of the other words, ask them to look for sounds they know in the word. Encourage them to sound out the words and help them read the words if necessary.
- After reading the story, ask the reader what Ken's first plan was.

Fun Activity

Plan how you would get to the Moon!

Ken's Plan

Ken can spot it.

Ken has a plan.

Ken can go up…

...and up!

Meg can go up...

...and up!

Book Bands for Guided Reading

The Institute of Education book banding system is a scale of colours that reflects the various levels of reading difficulty. The bands are assigned by taking into account the content, the language style, the layout and phonics. Word, phrase and sentence level work is also taken into consideration.

Maverick Early Readers are a bright, attractive range of books covering the pink to white bands. All of these books have been book banded for guided reading to the industry standard and edited by a leading educational consultant.

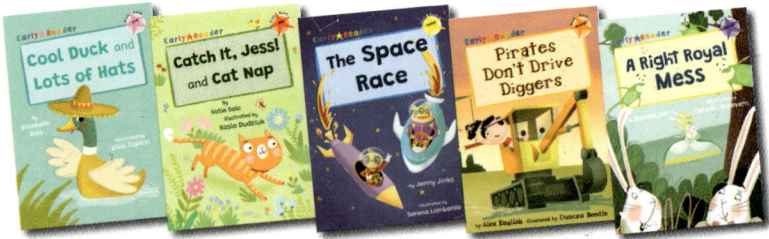

To view the whole Maverick Readers scheme, visit our website at www.maverickearlyreaders.com

Or scan the QR code above to view our scheme instantly!